Ladybird books are widely available, but in case of difficulty may be ordered by post or telephone from:
Ladybird Books – Cash Sales Department Littlegate Road Paignton Devon TQ3 3BE Telephone 0803 554761

A catalogue record for this book is available from the British Library

Published by Ladybird Books Ltd Loughborough Leicestershire UK
LADYBIRD and the device of a Ladybird are trademarks of Ladybird Books Ltd

Disney

Snow White
and the Seven Dwarfs

Ladybird

CHAPTER ONE

In a little kingdom graced with rolling hills, sparkling rivers and bountiful forests, there once lived a lovely young princess named Snow White. Snow White was not only kind, but beautiful as well. Her hair was deepest ebony, her skin the purest ivory.

Snow White's father, the King, was dead, and so she lived in the castle with her stepmother, the Queen. Although the Queen was also very beautiful, her beauty was only skin deep. Inside she was cold and heartless, and as evil as an ugly old witch.

The Queen was very jealous of Snow White's beauty. So much so that she forced the little Princess to dress in tattered rags and work long hours as a kitchen maid. The Queen thought that, disguised this way, Snow White's beauty could never rival her own. But that still wasn't enough to satisfy her vanity.

In a dark and forbidding part of the castle, the Queen kept a magic mirror. Every day she would stand before it and chant, "Magic mirror on the wall, who is the fairest of them all?"

And every day, the surface of the mirror would swirl like a dark whirlpool, and a grim face would appear, as if rising from the depths.

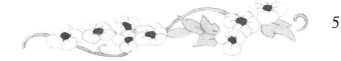

5

"*You* are the fairest one of all," the face would answer.

The Queen would smile and nod and feel content.

As time went on, however, Snow White's beauty became more and more apparent, in spite of the Queen's efforts to hide it. So it was that one day, when the Queen went to her dark, secret room and asked the mirror her usual question, it replied in its deep, sombre voice:

> *"Famed is thy beauty, Majesty,*
> *But hold — a lovely maid I see —*
> *Rags cannot hide her gentle grace.*
> *Alas, she is more fair than thee."*

The Queen stiffened in shocked surprise. Then her eyes narrowed, and she said, "Alas for *her*. Reveal her name."

And the face in the mirror answered:

> *"Lips red as a rose, hair black as ebony,*
> *skin white as snow…"*

"Snow White!" the Queen hissed.

*   *   *

At the very moment the Queen was consulting her magic mirror, Snow White was busy scrubbing the stone steps of the courtyard below. The work was hard, but Snow White did her job cheerfully. She sang as a flock of doves fluttered and cooed around her.

When she turned to draw water from a nearby well, Snow White gazed down at her reflection. She was startled to see another face next to hers.

"Oh!" she cried. Looking up, she saw a handsome young man in the fine dress of a prince standing beside her.

"Oh!" she cried again, backing away.

"Did I frighten you? I didn't mean to," the Prince said, with concern. "It's just that I heard such a lovely song as I was riding by."

Snow White was so flustered she couldn't speak. Finally, she ran towards the castle door, scattering the doves as she ran.

"Wait! Please don't go!" cried the Prince. "I'd like to talk to you!" But Snow White was already running up the castle's winding stone steps to a small balcony that overlooked the courtyard. When she reached the balcony, she peeped past the heavy curtains and looked down.

The Prince was still there, gazing up at the castle. He looked so handsome and seemed so kind that Snow White felt drawn to him.

Timidly at first, and then more boldly, she stepped closer to the balcony's edge.

When the Prince saw her, he couldn't keep from smiling. She was the most beautiful girl he had ever seen.

"Please come back," he urged. "I must get to know you."

Snow White smiled too, but she didn't move from the balcony.

As the Prince continued trying to persuade her to return, a dove flew up onto Snow White's hand. On impulse, the Princess kissed the dove and sent it down to the Prince.

Gently, the dove fluttered down and kissed the Prince. He blushed, and cried, "I shall never forget you!"

With that, Snow White withdrew into the dark castle.

* * *

Unknown to either Snow White or the Prince, the Queen had been watching this tender scene, and it filled her with even more anger and jealousy. She had been thinking of an evil plan. Now she made up her mind to carry it out.

The Queen called her chief huntsman to her throne. "Take Snow White far into the forest," she commanded him. "Find some secluded glade where she can pick wild flowers."

"Yes, your Majesty," answered the huntsman.

"And there, my faithful huntsman, you will *kill* her!"

Although the huntsman was a hardened man, he gasped and stared up at his Queen.

"But your Majesty," he cried, "the little Princess…"

"Silence!" snapped the Queen. "You know the penalty if you fail!"

"Yes, your Majesty," he said solemnly.

"To make doubly sure you do not fail," the Queen continued, glaring at the huntsman, "bring back her heart in this!" She held out an ornate red box. Its clasp was made of a jewelled dagger piercing a golden heart.

The huntsman took the box and slowly, sadly, nodded his head.

CHAPTER TWO

Snow White was soon wandering cheerfully through a lush green meadow, with the huntsman following close behind. She had been told that the Queen wanted some wild flowers for her table, and she was glad of the chance to go out into the countryside.

She was reaching down to pick a daisy when she suddenly saw a large, dark shadow falling over her. She whirled round in fright and then cringed in terror as she saw the huntsman looming over her, a sharp knife in his hand. She put her hands up to shield her face.

The huntsman came at her, his knife poised to strike. But at the last moment, his hand shook and his face fell.

"I can't do it," he cried, dropping to his knees. "Forgive me. I beg you, your Highness, forgive me."

"Why… why… I don't understand," stammered the frightened Princess.

"The Queen's jealous of you," the huntsman explained. "She's mad, she'll stop at nothing."

"The Queen?" said Snow White, her face growing pale.

"Yes," said the huntsman. "Now quick, child, run away. Hide!"

"But… where shall I go?" asked Snow White, her voice trembling.

"Into the woods – anywhere," said the huntsman, gesturing wildly at the thick forest beyond the meadow. "Now go! Run, and don't come back!"

Without another word, Snow White whirled and fled into the dark forest, stumbling blindly through dense trees and brush. As she ran, the things in the forest took on shapes and forms she had never before imagined. The branches of trees sprang to life around her. Rocks became hunched wild animals ready to rear up at a moment's notice.

Deeper and deeper into the forest she ran, until her path was blocked by an enormous black tree. Its gnarled trunk showed a grotesque and frightening face, and its thick branches reached out as if to grab and crush her.

Snow White screamed and stumbled into a nearby clearing. There she fell to the mossy ground, sobbing in terror until she was so exhausted she fell asleep where she lay.

CHAPTER THREE

The next morning, as the rays of the rising sun streamed down into the woods, curious eyes peeped out from the surrounding trees and bushes and stared at the sleeping girl.

Two fawns bobbed their heads and then cautiously picked their way forward. They were joined by a group of chattering chipmunks and bushy-tailed squirrels zig-zagging their way across the clearing. A rabbit family hopped out of its hiding place behind an old tree, followed by two black-eyed raccoons and a small flock of quail.

As half a dozen bluebirds fluttered down from the trees to join the other animals, one frisky little rabbit, bolder than the rest, hopped right up to Snow White. With a twitching pink nose it sniffed her hair. The Princess stirred and raised her head. "Oh!" she cried.

The rabbit seemed as startled as Snow White, and it bounded away. The other creatures also scurried for cover.

Snow White looked round. "Please don't run away," she said, "I won't hurt you."

As if they understood her, the forest animals reappeared. Snow White smiled at them.

"I'm awfully sorry," she continued. "I didn't mean to frighten you all. But you don't know what I've been through!"

The gentle creatures now came out and surrounded her. A baby bluebird perched on Snow White's hand, and she was heartened by its trust.

"I really feel much better now," she said. "I'm sure I'll get along somehow."

The animals all nodded in agreement.

"But I do need a place to sleep," Snow White said. "Perhaps you know where I can stay?" she asked the animals kindly.

A group of bluebirds chirped and twittered in reply.

"You do?" Snow White cried as she rose to her feet. "Will you take me there?"

In answer, the birds picked up the corners of Snow White's cape in their beaks and gently guided her along. Soon a small parade of animals was following Snow White and the birds as they made their way through the tangled woods. It was not long before they reached their destination.

The birds had taken Snow White to a snug little house nestled deep in the forest.

As soon as she saw the cottage in front of her, Snow White's spirits rose. It was a tiny house with white walls and a thatched roof. A small wooden bench stood outside, as if to welcome a weary traveller.

"Oh, it's adorable," Snow White murmured as she went closer. "Just like a doll's house. I like it here already!"

Snow White went to a window and wiped a clear circle in the grimy glass. "It's so dark inside," she said. "I don't think there's anyone at home."

Nevertheless, she went back to the doorway, which was framed by leafy vines on either side, and politely knocked on the thick wooden door. No one answered.

She turned to the animals. "I guess no one's at home," she said. Then she noticed that the door had opened slightly. With brisk steps she entered the tiny house and called, "Hello! May I come in?"

No one answered.

Snow White ventured further into the house, looking about in wonder. Everything was so *small*!

"What a sweet little chair!" she exclaimed. Then she saw that there were *seven* little chairs.

"Why, there must be seven little children living here," Snow White said to her animal friends.

As she looked round, Snow White could hardly believe her eyes. She realised that the whole cottage was untidy and full of dust and dirt. The sink was filled with unwashed dishes, there were dirty clothes everywhere, and the fireplace looked as if it hadn't been swept out in years!

"Why, they've never swept this room," said Snow White. "You'd think their mother would…" She paused as a thought occurred to her. "Maybe they have no mother," she said.

The animals nodded in sad agreement.

"Then they're orphans," Snow White said sorrowfully. "That's too bad."

She gazed round the untidy little house for a long moment, then announced, "I know what we'll do! We'll tidy up and surprise them! When they see how helpful I can be, perhaps they'll let me stay."

Again the animals nodded, as if they understood Snow White's meaning.

"Well, let's not just all stand here," she said with a good-natured laugh. "Let's get busy!"

And in no time at all, they did.

The squirrels scurried cheerfully round the cottage, sweeping the floor and dusting the furniture with their bushy tails.

The raccoons helped do the washing – they rubbed the clothes between their paws to get them sparkling clean.

The birds eagerly flew up into every nook and cranny in the ceiling, pulling down cobwebs and balls of dust with their strong beaks.

The deer and the rabbits pushed and pulled tables and chairs into their proper places.

Even the tiny chipmunks helped, carrying dirty cups, dishes and cutlery in their paws and mouths and putting them in the wooden sink to be washed.

With all the animals doing their share, the work went smoothly throughout the afternoon, as the sun slowly lowered to the west.

While all this was going on, the people who lived in the cottage were in the hills not far away, digging for jewels in a deep, dark mine. There were seven men in all, and they were dwarfs.

Despite their different personalities, the dwarfs all got on well together and worked side by side in perfect harmony. As they swung their picks and shovels, they sang a work song that echoed back to them through the caverns and tunnels of the mine.

Just as they started to sing another chorus, a clock in the mine struck five. One of the dwarfs looked up and cried, "Heigh-ho!" The others quickly collected their tools and marched out of the mine in single file.

They travelled along a well-worn path that wound through the wood and over rocky hills and small ravines. All the while, they whistled and sang, happy to be heading home after a good day's work.

*   *   *

Back at the cottage, Snow White and the animals looked round with pride at the sparkling-clean room. "Now let's see what's upstairs," Snow White said.

She led the way up the small wooden steps, and the animals followed. Upstairs she found a bedroom with seven little beds. A name was carved on each one.

"*Doc, Happy, Sneezy, Dopey…*" Snow White read aloud. "What funny names for children!" She laughed as she continued reading. "*Grumpy, Bashful, Sleepy.*"

Snow White yawned. "I'm a little sleepy myself," she murmured.

She lay down across three of the little beds and sighed. The animals gently pulled a blanket up to cover her and then, one by one, found cosy spots of their own.

Snow White's eyes closed, and soon she and the forest creatures were fast asleep.

CHAPTER FOUR

As Snow White and her friends slept, the sound of singing echoed through the forest. Before long it woke the animals. With tails twitching and noses quivering, they listened as the singing grew louder. It was the dwarfs, making their way home from work!

With startled leaps and bounds, the deer, squirrels, rabbits and chipmunks scampered out of the house and back into the wood, leaving Snow White still asleep on the tiny beds.

As the dwarfs approached the house, Doc pointed and said, "Look! Our house – the lit's light – I mean, the light's lit!"

The dwarfs immediately took cover behind a grove of thick pine trees. "Jiminy crickets!" they all cried at once.

"Door's open, chimney's smoking," said Doc. "Something's in there!"

"It… m-m-may be a ghost," stammered Happy.

"Or a goblin," whispered Bashful.

"It might be a – *a-achoo* – dragon," said Sneezy, his nose tickled by the scent of the pines.

The others glared at Sneezy and motioned to him to be quiet.

Grumpy scowled and said, "Mark my words, there's trouble a-brewing. Felt it coming all day. My corns hurt."

The dwarfs all looked at each other anxiously.

"What'll we do?" asked Sleepy. "I'm too sleepy to think."

"Let's sneak up on it!" Happy exclaimed.

"Yes!" said Doc. "We'll squeak up… er, I mean sneak up on it! Come on, hen… er, men! Follow me!" He led the way, holding up the lantern.

The dwarfs slowly and cautiously crept up to the house, one behind the other. When they got to the door, they filed in, quiet as mice, with Dopey in the rear. They were so close to each other they looked glued together. Suddenly Dopey slammed the door shut.

The dwarfs screamed and huddled against one another, expecting the worst. When they realised it was just Dopey, they put their fingers to their lips. "Shhh!" they hissed.

As the dwarfs tiptoed through the house, they noticed that things didn't seem quite as they had left them that morning.

"Look. The floor's been swept," said Doc.

Grumpy ran a finger along the top of a chair. "Huh. Chair's been dusted," he said in disgust.

"And our window's been washed," said Happy as he looked out at the forest beyond.

"Why, the whole place is clean!" Doc exclaimed.

"There's dirty work afoot!" growled Grumpy.

Just then Happy spied their big black pot bubbling over the fire. "Something's cooking," he said, sniffing, "and it smells good!"

Happy grabbed a spoon, ready to dip into the pot.

"Don't touch it, you fool!" shouted Grumpy, snatching the spoon from him. "It might be poison!"

Glancing nervously round the room, the dwarfs felt sure that some unknown and terrible creature had invaded their home. They could not imagine what it might be.

Looking down at them, some birds that had been hiding in the rafters began to twitter in mischievous delight. Suddenly the twittering turned to a shriek, and the dwarfs tumbled all over themselves in panic and fright.

When they finally settled down, Doc pointed upstairs. "Whatever it is, it's… up there," he said in a low voice.

"Yeah, in the bedroom," agreed Bashful.

"One of us has got to go down and chase it up… er, I mean, go up and chase it down," said Doc.

The dwarfs all nodded in agreement. Dopey nodded even more enthusiastically than the others – until he realised that everyone was staring at him. That could mean only one thing. They wanted *him* to lead the way!

Dopey tried to run, but the others grabbed him and pushed him up the stairs.

"D-don't be afraid," said Doc. "We're right behind you."

CHAPTER FIVE

Dopey took a deep breath and, holding his candle, climbed the darkened stairs to the bedroom. Slowly he opened the door. A long, low moan sounded through the darkness, and in the flickering light of the candle, Dopey saw something move under the covers.

Suddenly the candle went out, and with a yelp, Dopey burst out of the bedroom and pounded down the stairs.

"It's the creature!" the other dwarfs cried, falling all over each other as they tried to get out of the way. They yelled and screamed as they ran outside to hide behind the pine trees.

Meanwhile, Dopey, thinking the creature was right behind him, tried desperately to escape. In his haste, he crashed into a cupboard, and pots and pans came tumbling out over him. A large soup pot fell on his head, and he jammed his foot into another pot. When the other dwarfs saw him clanking and clumping towards them, they thought *he* was the creature, and they were even more terrified!

When the soup pot fell off Dopey's head and the others recognised him, they all calmed down. Then they began showering him with questions: "Did you see the creature? How big was it? Was it a dragon? Was it breathing fire? What *was* it doing?"

Dopey gestured that the creature was sleeping!

"A monster!" Doc cried. "Asleep in our beds!"

"Let's attack!" said Grumpy. "Before it wakes up!"

Doc agreed. "Hurry, men!" he shouted. "It's now or never!"

So the dwarfs marched bravely back to the house, determined to face whatever danger was there. Holding up their picks and clubs, they crept into the bedroom and right up to the beds where Snow White was sleeping.

Slowly, Doc pulled back the covers. The dwarfs were just about to strike when they saw Snow White. Stunned, they lowered their weapons and stood motionless.

At last Doc tried to speak. "Well… er… ah," he stammered.

"What is it?" asked Happy, gazing at the sleeping Princess.

"Why, I, it's… it's…" spluttered Doc, "it's a girl!"

Sneezy and Bashful both smiled.

"She's mighty pretty," said Sneezy.

"She's *beautiful*," said Bashful, blushing. "Just like an angel!"

All the dwarfs were captivated by Snow White. All but Grumpy, that is. "Angel, huh!" he said sourly. "She's a female. And all females is poison! They're full of wicked wiles!"

Doc told Grumpy not to speak so loudly, or he would wake the lovely girl up.

At that, Snow White's eyelids fluttered. Then she yawned and sat up. The dwarfs kept as still as they could.

"Oh dear," Snow White murmured to herself. "I wonder if the children are…" All at once her eyes opened and she saw the dwarfs.

"Oh!" cried Snow White, pulling the covers up around her. "You're not children at all. You're little men! How do you do?" She smiled politely.

"How do you do what?" asked Grumpy gruffly.

But Snow White was not put off by Grumpy's rudeness. "You can talk!" she said, pleased. "Let me see if I can guess your names."

She looked from one dwarf to the other, then pointed at Doc. "You must be Doc," she said.

"Yes," answered Doc politely.

Then she pointed at Sleepy, who was yawning. "I *know* you're Sleepy!" she said.

Sleepy replied with a bob of his head.

Dopey was gazing at her with his big blue eyes. "You must be Dopey," said Snow White.

Dopey nodded excitedly.

"And you must be Happy," Snow White said to Happy, who was grinning from ear to ear.

"That's right!" Happy chuckled gleefully.

She leaned forward to look at Bashful, who was hiding behind the others. "You're Bashful," she said gently.

"Yup," gulped Bashful, his face turning bright pink.

"Can you guess—*a-a-achooo!*—who I am?" asked Sneezy.

"I would say you're Sneezy!" said Snow White, giggling.

When Snow White finally got to Grumpy, she looked at his folded arms and stern expression and took the same pose herself. "And you must be Grumpy," she said in a deep voice.

Grumpy didn't answer her. He just turned to Doc and said, "We know who *we* are. Ask her who *she* is, and what she's doin' in our house!"

And so the dwarfs asked. Snow White explained who she was, and told them all about her terrible flight through the forest. "Please don't send me away," she begged them. "If you do, the Queen will kill me!"

"The Queen's an old witch!" said Grumpy. "And I'm warnin' you, if she finds Snow White here, she'll take revenge on all of us!"

"Oh, but she never will find me here," said Snow White. "And if you let me stay, I can keep house for you. I'm a good cook too!"

"A good cook!" cried the dwarfs, suddenly remembering their own hunger—and the pot bubbling on the fire. "She stays!" they all said together, in spite of Grumpy's glowering face.

CHAPTER SIX

Snow White went downstairs, followed by seven hungry dwarfs. She went over to the big pot, dipped a spoon in and tasted the contents. The dwarfs sniffed the air.

"It's soup – hooray!" they cried, making a dash for the dining table.

Snow White held up her hand. "Just a minute," she said. "Supper's not quite ready. You'll just have time to wash."

"Wash!" cried Doc.

"Wash?" said Bashful.

"Wash!" yelped Happy.

Grumpy threw down the spoon he had just picked up. "Huh! I knew there'd be a catch to it!" he said.

"Why wash?" asked Bashful. "We ain't goin' nowhere."

"Yeah," Doc chimed in. "And 'tain't New Year's or anything."

Snow White put her hands on her hips and raised her eyebrows. She looked at the dwarfs.

"Oh, perhaps you have washed already," she said with a knowing smile. "Recently?"

Doc nodded and said, "Yes, that's right. Perhaps we, er, yes, perhaps we have."

"When?" asked Snow White.

"Er, like you said, er, recently," replied Doc.

The other dwarfs murmured happily in agreement.

"Ohhhh," said Snow White with a suspicious look. *Recently.* Then let me see your hands."

The dwarfs lined up and, one by one, hesitantly showed Snow White their hands. Each pair was dirtier than the last.

"Oh, how shocking!" said Snow White. "Worse than I thought!"

She shook her head slowly. "I don't think that will do," she said to the shamefaced men. Then she pointed to the door. "March straight outside and wash, or you'll not get a bite to eat," she told them.

The dwarfs turned and slowly walked out of the house, moaning and groaning to themselves. All except Grumpy. He stood with his arms folded and his back to Snow White, with a sour expression on his face.

"Well, what about you?" asked Snow White. "Aren't you going to wash?"

Instead of answering, Grumpy just sulked.

"What's the matter?" Snow White teased. "Cat got your tongue?"

At that, Grumpy stuck out his tongue and headed out of the house in a huff.

The other dwarfs were gathered round the big wooden tub in the garden.

"Courage, men, courage," Doc urged.

"But the water's wet!" moaned Happy.

"Cold, too," complained Sneezy. "We ain't gonna *really* do it, are we?"

"Well… er," said Doc, struggling to think of a good reason, "it'll please the Princess."

Happy beamed at that. "Okay, then," he said, looking at the water doubtfully. "I'll take a chance for her!" He picked up the soap and leaned into the tub.

"Me too," the others agreed all together.

Grumpy sat on a barrel close by, listening to them. "You see?" he said. "Her wiles are beginnin' to work. I'm warnin' you – give 'em an inch, and they'll walk all over you!"

Doc looked sternly at Grumpy and told the other dwarfs not to listen to him. And with that, the men bravely began to scrub their faces, wash their hands, brush their teeth and comb their hair.

When they were finished, they looked at each other in amazement. They hardly recognised themselves.

"Hah!" cried Grumpy, still sitting on the barrel. "Bunch of old nanny goats. You make me sick! Next thing you know, she'll be tyin' your beards up in pink ribbons and smellin' you up with that stuff called, er, perfumy! Hah! What a fine bunch of water lilies!"

The dwarfs looked at Grumpy and then at each other. Then they all nodded.

"Get 'im!" Doc suddenly cried.

The dwarfs pounced on Grumpy and carried him over to the tub.

"Hey, let me loose, you fools!" Grumpy yelled as he squirmed to free himself.

But the dwarfs took no notice. Instead they dumped Grumpy right into the tub of soapy water and began to wash him thoroughly.

"Now scrub hard, men!" Doc told them. "It can't be denied, he'll look mighty cute as soon as he's dried!"

Grumpy fumed and fussed. "You'll pay for this!" he cried as he continued to struggle.

Suddenly they heard a loud *clang* as Snow White banged a spoon on the soup pot. "Supper!" she called.

"Supper!" the men shouted.

They all let go of Grumpy at once, and he fell back into the tub, spluttering and blowing bubbles as he gulped a mouthful of soapsuds.

Muttering and complaining, Grumpy finally got out of the tub and headed for the house. With a "Hmph!" he joined the other dwarfs, who were all at the table, eagerly awaiting their supper.

CHAPTER SEVEN

Back at the castle, the Queen stood once again before her magic mirror. But instead of the reply she expected, it said:

> *"Over the seven jewelled hills,*
> *Beyond the seventh fall,*
> *In the cottage of the seven dwarfs*
> *Dwells Snow White,*
> *Fairest one of all."*

Shocked and outraged, the evil Queen realised that she had been tricked. The huntsman had not brought back Snow White's heart in the box, but that of a forest animal. Snow White was still alive!

The Queen immediately began to think of another way to put an end to Snow White.

"*I'll* go to the dwarfs' cottage," she said to herself, "in a disguise so complete, no one will ever suspect it's me."

She swept down a flight of stone steps into her deep, dark dungeon. As she made her way across the gloomy chamber, scurrying rats squealed and ran for cover. Spiders, beetles and a host of other crawling things crept away at the sight of the evil Queen.

The only creature that didn't move was the Queen's pet raven, who watched her approach with unblinking eyes and an evil expression to match her own.

But the Queen took no notice of these things. She went straight to her book of black magic and flipped through its pages until she found what she wanted.

"Ah," she murmured, "a pedlar's disguise. Perfect!"

She went over to a table cluttered with phials and beakers filled with bubbling, smoking liquids. She selected one beaker and poured a steaming green liquid into a large goblet that was by her side.

"First, some mummy dust to make me old," she said, sprinkling a fine grey powder into the glass. "To shroud my clothes, the black of night." She added a drop of black liquid. "To age my voice, a drop of crow's blood." A deep red drop was added to the brew.

The Queen continued mixing her potion until she was satisfied that everything was exactly right. When she had finished, she held the goblet before her. The brew bubbled and hissed and spilled over the rim of the glass. She smiled grimly, and then with one quick motion she gulped down the foul liquid.

As soon as she had swallowed it, the Queen clutched her throat as if she were choking. The dungeon seemed to spin crazily round her, and a powerful wind rose up, rustling her robes and hair as if she were in the midst of a hurricane.

The Queen moaned as she shook violently and then crumpled over, as if the youth were being squeezed from her body.

52

As she quivered in the grip of the magic potion, her lustrous black hair began turning a dingy white, and her smooth face started to fold into hideous wrinkles. Her long, graceful fingers twisted into clawlike talons, and her elegant robe changed colour and shape until it was no more than a faded black rag.

Suddenly a flash of brilliant green light filled the dungeon. When it was gone, a haggard old witch stood in the place of the once-beautiful Queen. She shrieked in both triumph and agony as the awful transformation was completed.

The witch glanced in the mirror and cackled. "Yes, a perfect disguise," she croaked, and hobbled back to her book of spells.

"And now," she hissed, "I must plan a special sort of death for one so fair. What shall it be?"

She flipped through the pages of her book until something caught her eye. "Ah, yes!" she cried. "Just right. A poisoned apple!"

The witch's gnarled fingers traced the words, and she read aloud: *"One taste of the poisoned apple, and the victim's eyes will close for ever in the sleeping death."*

The old hag threw back her head and laughed long and loud, the sound echoing through the deep, dark dungeon like the shrieks of a hundred menacing crows.

CHAPTER EIGHT

As darkness settled over the forest, music rang out from the dwarfs' cottage while they entertained their new guest. Doc played the bass; Happy, Dopey and Sneezy yodelled and danced; Sleepy played the horn, lazily keeping time with his foot; and Bashful played the concertina and sang. Even Grumpy grudgingly joined in, playing the organ and yodelling in his low, growling voice. Snow White danced and sang along with them all.

When the music was over, Snow White sank into a chair and sighed contentedly. "That was fun," she said, her face flushed. "You were all so marvellous."

"Now you do somethin'," said Happy.

"Well, what shall I do?" asked Snow White.

"Tell us a story," piped up Sleepy.

All the dwarfs nodded in agreement. "Yes," they cried, "tell us a story!"

"A *true* story," added Happy.

"A lo-o-ove story," said Bashful with a blush.

Snow White looked at their eager faces and gathered the dwarfs round her. "Well," she began, "once there was a princess…"

"Was the Princess you?" Doc interrupted.

Snow White nodded. "And she fell in love with a prince…"

"Was it — *a-chooo!* — hard to do?" asked Sneezy.

Snow White shook her head and laughed. "It wasn't hard at all," she replied. "It was very easy. Anyone could see that the Prince was as good as he was charming." She looked away for a moment and sighed. "I knew he was the only one for me."

The dwarfs all began asking her questions at once.

"Was he big and tall?"

"Did he say he loved you?"

"Did he steal a kiss?"

"No," replied Snow White, "but he *was* romantic. I couldn't help being drawn to him. I had always known that some day I would meet someone I could love, and I did."

Then Snow White began to sing in her soft, sweet voice. And through the song, she poured out all of her heart's secret longings.

Just as the song was ending, the clock struck the hour.

"Oh my goodness," cried Snow White. "It's past bedtime. Go right upstairs, all of you." Playfully, she shooed the dwarfs out of the room.

"Hold on there, men," Doc cried. "The Princess will sleep upstairs in our beds."

"But where will you sleep?" asked Snow White.

"Why, er," answered Doc, "we'll be as bug as a snug in a rug — I mean, as snug as a bug in a rug down here."

"In a pig's eye," snapped Grumpy.

"Yep, in a pigsty — I mean, a pig's eye," echoed Doc. Then, realising what he had agreed with, he shook his head in dismay.

"We'll be comfortable, won't we, men?" he said to the dwarfs, looking especially at Grumpy.

"Oh yes," they answered, not sure whether they meant it or not.

Doc turned back to Snow White. "Go right up now, my dear," he said.

"Well, if you insist," replied Snow White. Then she smiled at them all and said good night.

In the bedroom, Snow White knelt beside one of the beds, closed her eyes and murmured, "Bless the seven little men who have been so kind to me, and… and may my dreams come true."

She started to rise, but quickly knelt down again.

"Oh yes," she added, "and please make Grumpy like me."

With that, she crept onto the beds and pulled up the covers.

CHAPTER NINE

Soon the whole house was still, with only the snoring of the seven dwarfs downstairs to break the silence. Outside, the forest, too, was quiet, its creatures having settled down for the night.

But there was someone who was wide awake and busily concocting a deadly gift—the evil Queen!

The old hag held a large apple on a string over a steaming cauldron. "Dip the apple in the brew," the Queen-witch chanted. "Let the sleeping death seep through."

The apple disappeared into the bubbling liquid, and when the witch pulled it out again a few seconds later, the brew dripped down the apple's sides, leaving the shape of a skull on its skin.

"Ah," sighed the witch. "On the skin, the symbol of what lies within. Now turn red," she commanded, "to tempt Snow White, to make her hunger for a bite."

At that, the apple turned a beautiful ruby red.

The witch held the apple in her hand and thrust it at her pet raven. "Have a bite?" she offered wickedly.

The bird shuddered and backed away from the poisoned treat.

The witch laughed in mischievous glee. "It's not for you, anyway," she cried. "It's for Snow White! When she breaks the tender peel to taste the apple in my hand," the hag went on, "her breath will still, her blood congeal. Then I'll be fairest in the land!"

Then the witch paused and frowned. "Wait," she said to the raven. "There may be an antidote. Nothing must be overlooked!"

She scurried over to her book of spells and flipped through it once again. Suddenly her bony fingers stopped at one of the pages.

"Ah, I was right," she said. "Here it is."

The witch started to read: *"The victim of the sleeping death can be revived only by love's first kiss."*

"Love's first kiss!" she hissed. "Bah! No fear of *that*! The dwarfs will think she's dead, and they'll bury her *alive*! Buried alive!" she screeched over and over, filled with wicked delight.

The witch grabbed a basket of ripe apples and gently placed the poisoned one among them. Then, with the basket of apples under her arm, she left the dungeon and descended the stone steps leading to the river that flowed beneath the castle.

She got into a small boat and began to row away into the night. A pale moon hung overhead, and shadows fell over her craggy features as she cackled, thinking of what was to come.

CHAPTER TEN

The next morning, Snow White awoke to see a bright yellow sun and blue sky peeping through the trees.

She had just enough time to give the men a hearty breakfast before they went off to work in the mine.

As the dwarfs were leaving, Doc said to Snow White, "Now don't forget, my dear. The old Queen's a fly… er, I mean, a sly one." He gently shook his finger at the Princess as he continued. "She's full of witchcraft. So beware of strangers!"

"Don't worry," answered Snow White. "I'll be all right."

One by one, she kissed the dwarfs on the forehead and said goodbye. And one by one they warned her to be careful.

Grumpy was the last to leave. Just before he joined the others, he cleared his throat and said, "Now I'm warnin' you. Don't let nobody or nothin' in the house."

Snow White looked down at him and smiled. "Oh, Grumpy, you *do* like me, after all!" she cried. With that, she planted a big kiss on his forehead.

"Hey, stop that mushy stuff!" Grumpy shouted, scowling as he broke away from Snow White's hug.

Grumpy marched away in a huff. But after a few steps, he turned round and gazed at Snow White with an adoring expression.

Snow White blew him a kiss, and he held his smile for a few more seconds. Then, suddenly, Grumpy realised what he was doing. He immediately scowled again and hurried off to join the others.

*   *   *

Not far from the cottage, the wicked witch was making her way through the forest.

"The little men will have gone by now," she cackled to herself. "She'll be alone. Alone, with a harmless old pedlar woman!"

She laughed long and loud, and two vultures in a nearby tree flapped away in alarm. But she quickly grew silent as she saw the cottage of the seven dwarfs come into view.

The animals and birds, who had welcomed Snow White, now sounded a warning as the old woman approached.

CHAPTER ELEVEN

As soon as the dwarfs had left, Snow White busied herself preparing food for their evening meal. After cutting up some carrots and potatoes, she decided to bake some gooseberry pies for dessert.

She was working by the window, just putting the finishing touches to one of her pies, when a dark shadow passed over her pastry board.

Looking up in surprise, Snow White saw an old woman peering into the house.

"All alone, my pet?" asked the old woman.

"Why… why, yes, I am, but…" Snow White answered hesitantly. She didn't know why, but she was a little frightened of the strange woman.

"The little men are not here?" asked the old woman.

"No, they're not," replied Snow White.

The old woman smiled. "Hmmm," she said. "Making pies?"

"Yes, gooseberry pies," answered Snow White, a bit more at ease. After all, this was only a harmless old pedlar woman.

The old woman grinned. "It's apple pies that make menfolk's mouths water," she said, taking the deep red apple from her basket. "Pies made from apples like these!" She held the apple up for Snow White to see.

"Oh, they do look delicious," said Snow White.

"Yes," murmured the old woman. "But wait until you taste one, dearie."

She held the poisoned apple out to Snow White. "Like to try one, hmmm?" she asked.

Snow White stepped back from the window, not sure of what to do. Her animal friends fretted and paced anxiously in the wood nearby. The birds, who had twittered in alarm at the sight of the old woman, now flapped their wings in helpless frustration as they saw Snow White get ready to take the tempting treat.

Suddenly, just as Snow White reached for the apple, the birds swooped down and knocked it from the old woman's hand. Then they fluttered round her, pecking at her head and body.

The witch waved her feeble arms and cried, "Oh, go away! Leave me alone!"

Snow White ran out of the house and shooed the birds away. "Stop it! Stop it right now!" she cried.

The birds flew back into the trees, where they perched restlessly.

"Shame on you," Snow White scolded, "frightening a poor old lady!"

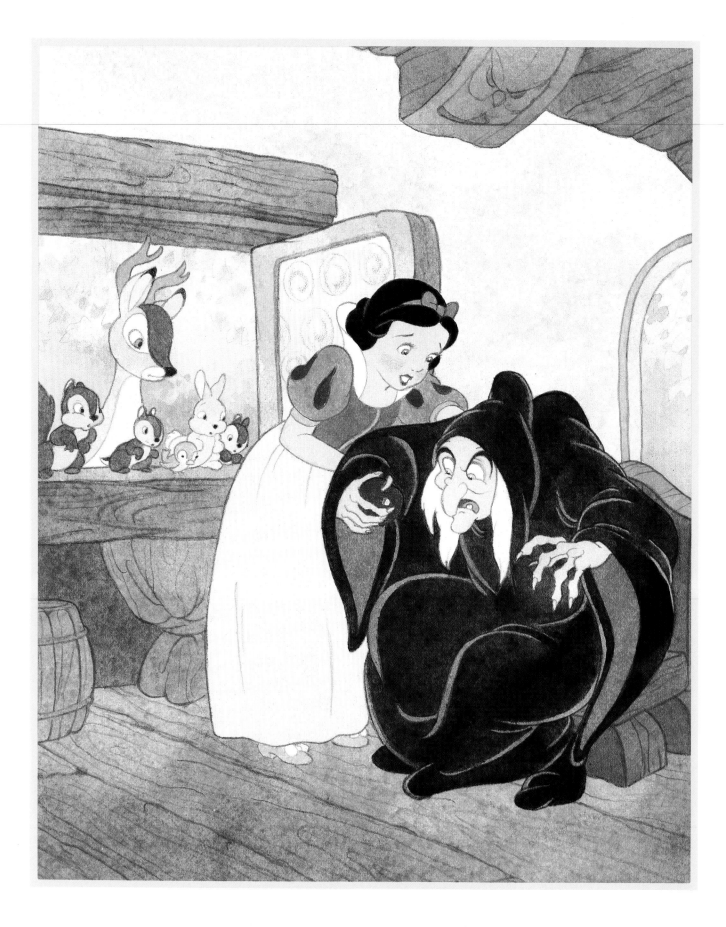

The birds hung their heads, not knowing what to do.

Snow White went to the old woman, who by now was on her hands and knees retrieving the apple.

The Princess helped the woman to her feet, then said, "I'm sorry. I don't know what has got into those birds. They're usually so gentle and kind."

The old woman nodded absently, then clutched at her chest and cried, "Oh, my poor heart!"

Snow White supported her by the arm and looked at her with concern.

"Please take me into the house," the old woman said. "Let me rest for a while. Perhaps I might have a glass of water?"

Snow White nodded and helped the old woman into the house.

The birds and animals rushed to the window to peep inside. They watched as Snow White helped the pedlar woman to a chair and gave her a drink of water.

When Snow White turned away for a moment, the old woman glowered at the birds and animals. They all backed away. Then, as if they'd all decided at once, they scampered off to find the seven dwarfs.

CHAPTER TWELVE

The animals crashed through thicket and brush as if a fire were chasing them. Finally they reached the mine. As soon as they saw the dwarfs, they began pushing and prodding them towards the cottage. The men thought the animals had gone mad.

"What ails these crazy critters?" cried Doc.

"They've gone plumb daffy!" yelled Bashful.

"Go on, git!" shouted Doc as a deer nudged him from behind. Turning to the others, he said, "These pesky critters won't stop!"

"'Tain't natural," cried Happy, flapping his arms to shoo the birds away.

"There's somethin' — *a-chooo!* — wrong," cried Sneezy.

Even Grumpy agreed. "They ain't actin' this way for nothin'," he grumbled.

Sleepy looked at everyone with half-closed eyes. "Maybe the old Queen's got Snow White," he said, stifling a yawn.

"*The Queen!*" cried Doc.

"*Snow White!*" cried the others.

Grumpy pounded his fist into his hand. "The Queen'll kill her! We've got to save her!" he cried. "Giddyap!" he shouted, as he hopped onto the back of a deer.

One by one, the dwarfs leapt onto the backs of the other deer and galloped towards their cottage. The strange parade hurtled through the forest, leaping over rocks and streams.

"Faster!" Doc urged them all. "We haven't got a moment to lose!"

*   *   *

Back at the cottage, the witch had pretended to recover her strength and was now having a friendly chat with Snow White.

She held up the poisoned apple once more. "Because you've been so good to old Granny," she said, "I'll share a secret with you."

Interested, Snow White leaned forward.

"This is no ordinary apple," the old woman said as she got to her feet. "It's a magic *wishing* apple!"

"A wishing apple?" said Snow White.

"Yes," answered the witch. "One bite and all your dreams will come true."

"Really?" said Snow White.

"Yes, girlie," the pedlar assured her. "Now make a wish and take a bite."

With a crooked smile, she held out the poisoned apple to Snow White.

CHAPTER THIRTEEN

The dwarfs raced through the forest, hoping to reach home and find Snow White safe. But time was running out.

"There must be something your little heart desires," the old woman was saying, still holding the apple in her hand. "Perhaps there is someone you love?"

"Well, there is someone," answered Snow White slowly.

"I thought so," the old woman said slyly. "Ha, ha, old Granny knows a young girl's heart."

She handed the apple to Snow White and patted her hand. "Now take the apple, dearie, and make a wish," she said.

Snow White gazed at the apple and said, "I wish…"

"That's it. Go on, go on," the witch urged.

"…that I will meet my Prince again, and that together we will travel to his kingdom," Snow White said more boldly.

"Fine," smiled the old woman. "Now take a bite – hurry! Don't let the wish grow cold!"

Snow White held the ruby red apple up and took a bite. As soon as she had done so, she tottered on her feet.

"Oh, I feel so strange!" she cried.

The old woman rubbed her hands in satisfaction as she chanted, *"Her breath will still."*

"Oh," cried Snow White, putting her hand to her forehead.

"Her blood congeal," hissed the old woman.

"Oh," moaned Snow White one last time, as she sank to the floor. There she lay, as still as death. The apple fell from her hand and rolled away.

Dropping all pretence now, the old woman threw back her head and howled with triumph. "It is done!" she cried. "Now I'll be the fairest in the land!" She turned and hurried out of the cottage and into the wood.

Suddenly a crack of lightning ripped across the sky, followed by a torrent of rain. It was as if the heavens themselves were angry at the witch for her wicked deed. But the old hag wasn't afraid. She had finally got rid of Snow White and could feel only joy at her achievement.

She cackled to herself as she hobbled through the wood, eager to return to her castle and her former self. She was just climbing over some rocks when she saw the seven dwarfs coming towards her.

"There she goes!" cried Grumpy. "After her!"

The witch scrambled up the rocky hill, crying out in frustration as she saw the dwarfs coming closer. Frightened and desperate, she climbed further out, onto a rocky ledge which overhung a deep ravine.

The wind and rain lashed at the witch's face and clothing. As she looked about wildly, she realised she was cornered.

"I'm trapped!" she cried. "The meddling little fools!"

She picked up a broken tree limb and, using it as a lever, started to pry loose a huge boulder that was perched on the ledge. Her magic now gave her the strength of ten men, and the boulder started to teeter back and forth.

"I'll fix you! I'll fix you!" she cried out to the dwarfs. "I'll crush your bones!"

"Look out!" cried Grumpy. "She's going to roll that boulder right over us!"

The witch laughed as the boulder started to come loose. But just as it was about to roll down onto the dwarfs, a bolt of lightning struck the rocky ledge. In an instant, it shattered and fell away, carrying the witch and the boulder with it. The witch gave out a long, horrifying shriek as she tumbled to the jagged rocks below.

Cautiously, the dwarfs approached the edge of the broken ledge and looked down. They couldn't see the witch, but when they saw two greedy-eyed vultures swoop down, they knew she was gone for ever.

But when they finally reached their cottage, they found Snow White lying motionless on the floor.

"She... she's dead," cried Sleepy.

The others nodded sadly. The Queen had won, after all.

CHAPTER FOURTEEN

The dwarfs could not bear to bury the Princess, so they fashioned a delicate coffin of gold and glass and gently placed Snow White in it. They carried the coffin to a peaceful glen in the wood, where they put flowers all round it. And there Snow White remained, as beautiful as ever, with the dwarfs lovingly keeping vigil beside her.

One morning the following spring, the dwarfs came to sit by the coffin as usual. They opened the glass top and put a bouquet of fresh flowers in Snow White's hands. Then they knelt beside the coffin.

They were surprised to see a handsome prince ride into the clearing on a white horse. They didn't know it, of course, but he was the very same young man who had first met Snow White at the well. He had heard about the beautiful maiden who slept in the glass coffin, and he was eager to see if it was the same Princess he had once met.

As he approached the coffin, the Prince saw that it *was* the same girl. Sadly, he knelt by the coffin and bowed his head. When he rose, he bent over the still form and gave Snow White one farewell kiss. To his surprise and joy, Snow White's eyes fluttered open.

She was alive! Love's first kiss had broken the witch's spell!

Snow White slowly sat up and smiled. She looked as if she had just awoken from a good night's sleep. When she saw the Prince, her eyes lit up in surprise and delight, and she held out her arms to him. The Prince embraced her and lifted her up.

For a moment the dwarfs stood still, in silent disbelief. Then, overcome with joy, they threw their hats in the air and cheered and cheered.

When the dwarfs had finally calmed down, Snow White went over and looked at each one of them fondly. "You have been good, kind friends," she said softly, "and I shall never forget you."

One by one, Snow White kissed the dwarfs on the forehead.

"Goodbye, Princess," they called as the Prince lifted Snow White onto his horse.

"Goodbye!" she called back.

The Prince took the reins of his steed and slowly led it away.

"Goodbye!" Snow White called out once more, as she and the Prince slowly disappeared from view.

When Snow White and the Prince had gone, the dwarfs looked at each other and smiled. They would miss her, but they knew that Snow White's wish had finally come true. She had found her true love, and she would live happily ever after. That made them happy too—even Grumpy!